This book belongs to:

_____

For Klaus, my publisher...
fortunately

This paperback edition first published in 2018 by Andersen Press Ltd.

First published in Great Britain in 2010 by Andersen Press Ltd.,

20 Vauxhall Bridge Road, London SW1V 2SA.

Copyright ©Michael Foreman, 2010.

The right of Michael Foreman to be identified as the

author and illustrator of this work has been asserted by him

in accordance with the Copyright, Designs and Patents Act, 1988.

All rights reserved.

Colour separated in Switzerland by Photolitho AG, Zürich.

Printed and bound in Malaysia.

1   3   5   7   9   10   8   6   4   2

British Library Cataloguing in Publication Data available.

ISBN 978 1 78344 740 4

Fortunately, Unfortunately

MICHAEL FOREMAN

ANDERSEN PRESS

"Milo! Milo!"

It was Mum.

"Granny has left her umbrella here.
Can you take it round to her house, please?"

Fortunately,

it was a lovely day

and Milo liked going to Granny's house because she always had cakes for tea.

Fortunately,

he had Granny's umbrella...

Unfortunately,

a dark cloud appeared and it soon began to rain...

Unfortunately,

he didn't look where he was going...

Fortunately,

the umbrella was

like a parachute...

Unfortunately, there was a whale...

Fortunately,
the umbrella kept Milo afloat inside the whale –
and there was a wonderful pirate ship...

Unfortunately,
the pirate captain was not very friendly...

Fortunately, he was not very good at sword fighting either...

Unfortunately, his pipe fell on the gunpowder...

Fortunately, Milo flew out of the whale's mouth...

Unfortunately, he was caught up in a TYPHOON...

... and dropped into a
lost world at the top of
a volcano.

Fortunately, he splashed down in the blue waters of a lake...

Unfortunately,
it was full of wild dinosaurs...

Fortunately, the volcano erupted and Milo was thrown

up into the sky again...

Unfortunately, he was captured by an alien spaceship...

Fortunately, the aliens were very tiny – and friendly...

Unfortunately,
they were hijacked by a bigger alien spaceship

and these aliens were huge and very unfriendly...

Fortunately, they were just full of hot air and easily popped...
like big smelly balloons...

"Go! Go!" the huge aliens cried.

Fortunately, the little aliens flew Milo all the way to...

Granny's house...

Unfortunately, Granny's umbrella was now a bit of a mess.

"What have you done to my umbrella?

Look at the state of it!"

Fortunately, it was full of pirate treasure...

Unfortunately, there was also a little alien...

Fortunately, his friends came back for him...

And they all had tea...

Unfortunately...

"Come on, shipmates!
The old lady has got
our treasure..."